Graveyard Diaries

TO WEREWOLF OR NOT TO WEREWOLF

magic
wagon

by Baron Specter
illustrated by Setch Kneupper

visit us at www.abdopublishing.com

Printed in the United States of America, North Mankato, Minnesota.
052012
112013
 This book contains at least 10% recycled materials.

Text by Baron Specter
Illustrations by Setch Kneupper
Edited by Stephanie Hedlund and Rochelle Baltzer
Interior layout and design by Neil Klinepier
Cover design by Neil Klinepier

Library of Congress Cataloging-in-Publication Data

Specter, Baron, 1957-
  To werewolf or not to werewolf / by Baron Specter ; illustrated by Setch Kneupper.
      p. cm. -- (Graveyard diaries ; bk. 4)
  Summary: Jared Jensen and his fellow zombie hunters think there is a werewolf loose in the cemeteries of Marshfield, but is it connected with the strange boy called Rudy or not?
  ISBN 978-1-61641-901-1
  1. Werewolves--Juvenile fiction. 2. Cemeteries--Juvenile fiction. 3. Missing children--Juvenile fiction. [1. Werewolves--Fiction. 2. Cemeteries--Fiction. 3. Lost children--Fiction. 4. Mystery and detective stories.] I. Kneupper, Setch, ill. II. Title.
  PZ7.S741314To 2012
  813.6--dc23
                                        2011052781

CONTENTS

Woodland Cemetery

Jared's House

Marshfield Grove

Barry's House

MARSHFIELD

Chapter 1:
That's No Muskrat

Jared Jensen woke from a peaceful dream. He heard a splash. Something was swimming in the pond.

His friend Stan Summer was snoring in a sleeping bag. Jared smacked Stan's arm.

"What?" Stan asked, shooting up.

The inside of the tent was very dark. Jared pushed aside a soda can and an empty potato chip bag. He found his flashlight and turned it on.

"I heard a splash down in the pond," Jared said.

"So what?" Stan said. "It was probably a duck."

"Just listen," Jared said. "There it is again."

Jared unzipped the tent flap and looked out. The night air was cool for August. They were on top of a hill in Woodland Cemetery. There was a small pond at the bottom of the hill.

"It's just a muskrat," Stan said.

There was another splash—a loud one.

"That's no muskrat," Jared said. "It's something big. Let's go take a look."

"It's one o'clock in the morning!" Stan said.

"Right," Jared said. "What could be better than being out in the middle of the night? Let's go."

Stan sighed. He tugged his hiking boots on. "We'll get bitten up by bugs," he said. "Or attacked by a bear."

Jared had pulled on a blue sweatshirt that

said GHOST CROSSING. He was already crawling out of the tent.

Jared stood and looked toward the pond. Someone—or some thing—was swimming. Jared could hear the steady movements.

"Hurry up," he said to Stan.

Woodland Cemetery was hilly and covered with forest. Jared's backyard went right to the edge of the graveyard. He spent a lot of time out here. He and Stan liked to camp in the summer. They usually pitched a tent in this spot. It was far from the road or any houses. Most of the gravestones were on the other side of the hill.

There were four graveyards in the town of Marshfield. All of them were haunted. Jared and Stan and some others had formed a group called the Zombie Hunters. They often battled ghouls in the graveyards.

"Stay quiet," Jared said as they walked

down the hill. They had to go slowly to avoid roots and rocks. The moon was not up yet, so there was not much light. Just the beams from their flashlights.

The pond was surrounded by woods. Jared climbed onto a boulder that was half in the water and half out. Whatever was swimming was near the other side of the pond.

Stan climbed onto the rock, too. Jared jumped when he heard someone singing. The voice was coming from the water. "Something evil's lurking in the dark," it sang.

Jared held up his light and scanned the water. The pond was about the size of a basketball court.

"Who's there?" shouted the voice from the water.

Jared shut off the light.

The voice called again. "What do you want?" He began to swim toward the boys.

Jared put the light on again. "We were camping," he called. "We heard you swimming."

As the swimmer got closer, Jared could see that he was a few years older than the boys. A teenager. He swam very quickly and reached the boulder in a few seconds.

The swimmer stood in the shallows and shook the water from his dark hair. He was small and lean, but he looked strong. He was wearing only a pair of gray shorts. His eyebrows were dark and thick. They met in the middle above his nose, making one long brow.

"Who are you?" the swimmer asked.

Jared shined the light on his own face. "Jared and Stan. We live over that way." Jared waved his hand up the hill.

The teenager nodded. "I'm Rudy."

"Funny time to be swimming," Stan said. "What's up with that?"

"I always swim at night," Rudy said.

"There's no one around to bother me." He frowned. "Not usually."

"Sorry about that," Jared said. "There's a pool in the park, you know. You can swim there for free if you live in this town."

Rudy just shrugged.

"Do you?" Jared asked.

"Do I what?"

"Do you live in this town?"

Rudy looked back across the pond. "No. I live out here."

"In the woods?" Stan asked.

"Yeah."

"You can't live in the woods," Jared said. "Where do you sleep?"

"I don't sleep much," Rudy said. "I'm busy at night."

"Doing what?" Stan asked.

"Hunting. Eating."

"Hunting what?" Stan asked.

"Squirrels. Rabbits. A deer when I can catch a young one."

"You couldn't catch a deer," Jared said. "Even the fawns are too fast for a human to run down."

Rudy smiled slightly. "Yes," he said. "For a normal human."

"You aren't normal?" Jared asked.

Rudy turned and dived into the water. He took several strokes before looking back. "I'm very fast," he said, "and very quiet."

Rudy swam to the other end of the pond. Then he stepped into the woods and was gone.

"Very strange," Jared said.

"He's a liar," Stan replied. "Nobody lives in these woods."

"Maybe in the summer he could," Jared said. "But he'd freeze any other time of year." A bug buzzed by his ear, and he swatted at it. "And he'd get eaten alive."

Jared shined the light up the hill. He could see the tent up there. It was a square, green tent. Plenty of room for two campers.

Jared's stomach growled. Breakfast was a long way off. "Do we have any food left in the tent?" he asked.

"There are a few pretzels," Stan said. "They're a little soggy. I spilled some soda."

"Sounds awful," Jared said. He climbed off the boulder. The ground was damp here by the pond. It squished under his sneakers as he started walking up the hill.

"That guy was weird," Stan said. "Do you know that song he was singing?"

"It was 'Thriller' by Michael Jackson," Jared said.

"It sounded familiar," Stan said. "You don't think he'd come to the tent, do you?"

"Why would he do that?"

"Just to try to scare us," Stan said. "To prove that he's tough."

"He'll never find us unless he has a light," Jared said. "It's too dark out here."

Stan stopped and looked around. "What if he's following us?"

"We'd hear him."

"He said he's very quiet."

Jared bent to pick up a rock in the path. Then he grabbed another. "Get some rocks," he said. "Just in case."

They reached the tent and zipped up the flap. Jared settled into his sleeping bag.

He kept the rocks where he could grab them quickly.

"Let's go to sleep," he said.

But neither boy shut his eyes. They listened to every sound outside the tent. Branches moved in the breeze. Crickets chirped.

Jared knew that he wouldn't be getting anymore sleep. He pulled the top of his sleeping bag over his head and turned on his flashlight. He rolled onto his stomach and took out his small notepad. He liked to keep track of strange events. This was definitely one of them. So he started to write.

Jared's Journal: Wednesday, August 4. About 1:30 a.m.

It was a peaceful night until a little while ago. A strange guy was swimming in the pond. He says he lives in these woods. I would have seen him before if that was true. Maybe he's just passing through the area. But we need to keep a watch on him. This is our place. We camp here, we hike here, we ride our bikes here. I don't want some creepy guy living out here, too.

A scrambling sound in the woods made Jared sit up. Something was being chased. Jared could hear a small animal bounding through the trees. Something much larger was running just as fast. Its footsteps were loud as it crashed through the woods.

And then there was a scream.

A high-pitched, terrified scream.

Chapter 2:
A Full Moon

"Don't turn on your light," Jared whispered.

"Why not?" Stan asked. He had crawled out of his sleeping bag right after the scream. He pulled open the tent flap.

"I don't want that guy knowing where we are."

"You had your light on!"

"It's off now," Jared said.

Stan sat back on the tent floor. "What do you think was screaming?"

"Not a person," Jared said. "It sounded

too wild. Like a panther or something."

"There aren't any panthers around here," Stan said. "Probably just a rabbit. I've heard that they scream sometimes."

"When?" Jared asked.

"When they're in pain!"

They sat quietly and listened. There was no more screaming. "It's probably dead," Jared said.

"Maybe that guy caught it and bit right through it."

"Rudy?" Jared shook his head. "How could he catch a rabbit in the dark? And with his bare hands?"

"He said he could."

Jared picked up the rocks. He stepped out of the tent again. He pointed toward the deep woods. "It came from over there," he said.

Stan looked that way, too. He pointed toward the sky. The moon had come up. It was shining brightly over the top of the next hill. The boys could see their shadows. There was much more light than before.

Something was moving in the woods nearby. It walked slowly and steadily.

Jared froze. By the light of the moon he could see what was coming. A dark animal on four legs was weaving its way through the trees. It had a long tail and shiny yellow eyes.

"Is that a bear?" Jared whispered.

"I think it's a wolf," Stan answered.

"There aren't any wolves around here."

"There might be now."

The animal moved faster down the hill. Then there was a splash. Jared could hear it swimming in the pond.

And then he heard singing again. It was Rudy. "It's close to midnight . . ."

Jared could see the entire pond by the light of the moon. There was no wolf in the water. There was only Rudy swimming on his back, looking up at the moon. He was singing that Michael Jackson song.

"It's way after midnight," Jared said. "It's starting to get light out."

"That light is from the moon," Stan said. He pointed toward the pond. "Do you think we should warn him?"

"About what?" Jared asked.

"That wolf that we saw," Stan said. "It was headed straight for the pond."

Jared shrugged. "I don't think that wolf will bother him."

"Why not?"

"I think he *is* the wolf," Jared said. "A wolf dove into the pond. Then he came up as a guy—*that guy*."

Stan let out a whistle. "You think he's a werewolf?"

Jared nodded. "It adds up. He doesn't sleep. He eats raw animals that he kills."

"Are you saying that he can turn into a wolf whenever he wants?" Stan asked.

"It looks like it."

"I thought that was out of their control," Stan said. "Werewolves don't want to become wolves. It just happens. Like when the full moon comes up."

Jared looked at the moon. It was getting higher in the sky. "I read that some werewolves can turn from human to wolf whenever they want."

They heard more splashing. And then Rudy began to sing again.

Stan said, "Do you think he swims to wash off the animal blood?"

"Wouldn't you?"

"Yeah," Stan said. "That's pretty gross. I can't imagine eating a raw rabbit."

"Or killing one with your bare hands," Jared said. "And ripping it apart to eat it."

"Yuck," Stan said. "Lots of blood and guts."

Jared stared at the swimmer in the pond for a moment. "We should probably get out of here," he said.

"You mean go home?" Stan asked.

The boys had always stayed out all night when camping. They were proud of that. They were eleven and twelve, but they had stayed in the tent through rainstorms and strong winds. Once they'd seen a bear outside the tent. And some nights they'd heard things they couldn't explain. Eerie voices and laughter.

So why would a werewolf make them leave?

"He could kill us," Jared said.

"No, he couldn't," Stan said. "That guy isn't much bigger than we are."

"He couldn't kill us," Jared said. "But his werewolf form might."

Stan took a step back. "He's not hungry," Stan said. "Not if he just ate a rabbit."

Jared looked at the rocks in his hands. "We're not chickening out," he said. "But we need help. We'll come back tomorrow night with the other Zombie Hunters. And more weapons."

"Okay," Stan said. "I guess. But let's leave the tent."

"Yeah, leave it," Jared said. "We'll come back for it in daylight. For now, we can get some sleep at my house."

Jared started walking toward home. He looked back several times. He could still hear the singing from the pond.

And then he heard a loud, evil-sounding laugh.

Jared and Stan started to run. They'd had enough of this for one night.

Chapter 3:
Zombie Hunters' Meeting

Jared's Journal: Wednesday, August 4.
4:47 a.m.

    We made it home safely. Stan's already asleep. I'll need to sleep soon, too. I think we'll be up all night tonight. We need to put an end to this quickly. The werewolf may be the most dangerous thing we've ever met. They get a taste for blood, and then they come after people. We need to stop him now before he takes any human victims. But how do we get rid of him? I have no idea.

Time to get some shut-eye. If I can.

That afternoon, Jared and Stan got a hold of the other Zombie Hunters. They made plans to meet at the Grotto for pizza. They needed to discuss the werewolf.

The Grotto was on Main Street. It was a small, casual place. Jared and Stan went there a lot for pizza and soda.

Amy Martinez was waiting when they got there. She lived right near Stan on the edge of Hilltop Cemetery. She was very clever and was good at out-smarting ghosts.

Mitch Morris and Barry Bannon arrived a few minutes later. Mitch lived by Evergreen Cemetery and knew a lot about vampires. Barry's home was by Marshfield Grove Cemetery. He was an expert on zombies.

None of the Zombie Hunters had ever met a werewolf before last night. But they'd heard a lot about them.

"They have a huge thirst for blood," Barry said. He poured some soda into a glass and took a big gulp. "Almost like a vampire."

"And their sense of smell is strong," said Mitch. "A hundred times better than a human's." He picked up a slice of pizza from the tray and held it to his nose. He inhaled deeply and smiled.

"So, how do we stop this one?" Jared asked. "Before he bites somebody? Anyone infected by a werewolf bite becomes a werewolf, too."

"Unless the person who gets bitten dies first," said Stan. "What else do we know? Every bit of information can be useful."

Amy cleared her throat. "This might be worthless," she said, "but I read that werewolves can't climb trees."

"I don't know about that," Jared said. "This guy last night was fast and strong. He could easily climb a tree."

"Yes, as a human," Amy said. "But not as a wolf."

"Well, that's obvious," Stan said.

"Just keep it in mind," Amy said. "You asked for any information we had."

"That's right," Jared said. "What else do we know?" He took a bite of pizza and stared out toward Main Street. A few teenagers were hanging out on a bench. An old man walked by with a little dog.

Mitch described how a person became infected by a werewolf. After being bitten, he would have a high fever for a few days. Then he would develop thick hair. Soon he would turn into a wolf.

"But sometimes they turn back into people," he said. "And when the fever returns, they switch into wolves again."

"And what makes the fever come back?"

Stan said.

"I think it's the moon," Amy replied. "It was almost full last night."

"It doesn't have to be full," Mitch said. "But a bigger moon has a bigger effect. So this week the moon is powerful."

"It will be full tonight," Jared said. "So this is a great night to try to stop him."

Jared grabbed his soda glass and lifted it to his lips. But he saw something that made him spit the soda back. He couldn't believe who was entering the restaurant.

The door opened and in walked Rudy. He was dressed in a black T-shirt and jeans. His hair was mussed up, but he looked like a normal human. No extra hair.

Jared nudged Stan.

"That's him," Stan said.

"Who?" asked Amy.

"It's the werewolf," Stan said.

Rudy had walked to the counter. He ordered a meatball sandwich. "With extra sauce," he said.

Jared leaned forward and whispered to the others. "He's the one who was swimming in the pond last night. He turned into a wolf."

"And killed a rabbit," added Stan.

Rudy sat at a nearby table. He took a big bite of his sandwich. Tomato sauce squeezed out of the sandwich. It dripped down his chin.

Jared called over to Rudy. "You'll need another swim in the pond."

Rudy stared at Jared. "What are you talking about?" he asked.

"You'll have to wash off that sauce in the pond," Jared said.

Rudy frowned. He took another bite. With his mouth full, he said, "What pond?"

"In the cemetery."

Rudy turned away and mumbled. "I don't know who you are. And I don't know what you're talking about."

Jared looked at Stan and laughed. He took another piece of pizza. "That's him," Jared said. "Nobody else has eyebrows like that."

When Rudy got up to leave, Jared tried again. "It's us," he said. "Jared and Stan."

Rudy stopped walking, but he didn't say anything.

"We met last night," Jared said. "In the graveyard."

"Get lost," Rudy said. "I wasn't in any graveyard last night." He walked to the door and went out to the street.

"Weird," Mitch said. "Are you sure that was him?"

"Definitely," Jared replied.

"Maybe he has a twin," Barry said.

Jared shrugged. "Maybe. Or maybe he's lying again."

They talked about werewolves some more.

"They're also called 'shape shifters,'"

Mitch said. "That means they go back and forth from human to wolf. You can deal with them when they're human. But as wolves, they'll bite you. And sometimes kill you, if they're hungry."

Amy said she'd help if she could, but she wouldn't be able to camp out overnight. They all decided to meet at nine o'clock at her house.

A while later, Rudy came back into the Grotto. He didn't say a word. Instead, he walked over to the jukebox and put in some coins. Then he left the restaurant.

"He just wasted money," Jared said. "He didn't even wait to hear the song."

And then Jared knew why. The first notes of the song began. It was "Thriller."

"I told you it was him," Jared said. "That's his theme song."

"How do you know?" Amy asked.

"Because he was singing it last night in the pond."

Chapter 4:
The Unexplainable

Jared spent the early evening on the Internet, looking for werewolf information. The most reliable Web sites said stories about werewolf encounters were usually exaggerations. A suspected werewolf might have rabies, or an infection that caused wild behavior. A defect in the brain could cause the same symptoms.

But some cases were unexplainable. *Like this one,* Jared thought.

Jared's Journal: Wednesday, August 4. 8:19 p.m.

Not sure what to do yet. We can't kill him. He's a human being. We'd be charged with murder. But unless we figure out a way to stop him, we might become murder victims ourselves. This won't be easy.

None of us has had to deal with a werewolf before. They're dangerous because they move quickly and have great strength. We'll have to stick close together and be ready. One bite from a werewolf can change your life forever. Or end it!

Jared left the house and headed for Stan and Amy's neighborhood. It wasn't quite dark yet. All he had to do was walk through Woodland Cemetery. A path connected it with Hilltop Cemetery.

The walk was peaceful in daylight. But tonight it seemed spooky. That werewolf could attack without warning.

Jared started to run. He passed through Stan's yard, then up to Amy's house.

Amy was sitting on the front steps.

"Have any good ideas for us?" Jared asked.

"Besides being careful?" Amy replied.

Jared smiled. "I know that. But how can we get rid of this werewolf?"

Amy shook her head. "I wish I knew," she said. She looked up at the sky. "It's a clear night. But the moon won't be up until around twelve o'clock."

"That's good to know," Jared said. "I think the moon is what changes him from human to wolf. So we may be safe until it rises. Maybe we can trap him before then."

"Is that the plan?" Amy asked. "To trap him?"

Jared shrugged. "We don't have a plan," he said. "But trapping him might be a good idea."

"You'd need a big net," Amy said.

"Right," Jared said. "That's probably not a good idea. Especially since we don't have a net."

"And what would you do with him if you caught him?" Amy asked. "You can't just tie him up and leave him. He's a person."

"I know," Jared said. "And so far he hasn't hurt anyone. So I guess we'd better just keep an eye on him. And be ready to deal with him if we have to."

"Why do you have to?" Amy asked. "Why not just leave him alone? You guys don't have any reason to be out in the cemetery all night."

"But we want to," Jared said. "Besides, I like to stay out in the cemetery some nights. We camp there all the time. We would never be safe if there was a werewolf running loose."

Stan came walking up the street. He was carrying a coil of thick rope.

"What's that for?" Amy asked.

"We might have to lasso the werewolf," Stan said.

"Do you know how to do that?" Jared asked.

Stan looked at the rope and frowned. "No."

"That's okay," Jared said. "The rope might come in handy anyway."

"That's what I figured," Stan said. "What else should we bring?"

"Mitch and Barry said they'd get some baseball bats and an axe," Jared said.

"Maybe you should make some torches," Amy said. "Something you can light on fire."

"Why?" Stan asked. "Are werewolves afraid of fire?"

"I don't know," Amy said. "But fire can stop anything. If I was a wolf, I wouldn't attack anything that had a torch. Would you?"

Stan went back to his garage and found

two broomsticks. He put full rolls of paper towels over the ends of the sticks. Then, he secured them with duct tape. The rolls would burn for several minutes when lit.

Mitch and Barry soon arrived. The Zombie Hunters decided to stash their weapons in the tent.

The sun was nearly down, but they still had some light to see by. They walked through Hilltop Cemetery, carrying the rope and bats and things. Then they crossed into the forest that led to Woodland Cemetery.

Jared felt uneasy. He kept glancing around. Each time he heard a branch move, his stomach tightened. Something wasn't right.

"I feel an evil presence," he said. "Like something bad is going to happen."

"Don't be a baby," said Mitch, who always acted tough. "We've faced worse things than a werewolf before. That guy we saw at the pizza place didn't look very big. We could handle him easily."

"Sure we could," said Jared. "But it isn't him I'm concerned about. At least not as a human. When he turns into a wolf it will be a different story."

Mitch smirked. He swung a baseball bat slowly. "It will be the end of the story for him."

They reached the top of the hill. The campsite was empty.

"Where's the tent?" Stan asked.

"It was right here!" Jared said. "Somebody took it."

Jared turned on his flashlight and ran the beam along the ground.

"What's this?" said Amy. She bent and picked up a piece of green fabric.

Jared took the fabric. "That's part of the tent," he said. He could see other scraps of it on the ground and hanging from trees. Someone had shredded the tent to bits.

There were hundreds of pieces. None of the pieces were bigger than a square of toilet paper.

"It looks like a bomb hit it," Barry said. "Or a tornado."

Jared shined his light on a big set of paw prints. There were many of them in the dirt. They looked like they'd come from a large dog. Or a wolf.

"No tornado," Jared said. "Our werewolf friend paid a little visit. Good thing we weren't here at the time. I think he was looking for human blood!"

Chapter 5:
Lying, Tent-wrecking Jerk

Jared and Stan leaned against a boulder and stared at the bits of tent. Mitch and Barry had left to walk Amy home. They'd be back soon. The night was very dark.

Jared swatted at a mosquito. "We should make a fire," he said. "It will keep away the bugs."

"Good idea," Stan said.

They'd made campfires here before, so they already had a ring of stones. They gathered some twigs and bark. It hadn't rained for a couple of weeks, so everything was dry. The fire started quickly. They added bigger pieces of wood.

The fire was warm and bright. Jared took out his notebook.

Jared's Journal: Wednesday, August 4. 9:55 p.m.

The stupid werewolf wrecked my tent. It cost me more than $100 to buy that tent. I'm mad. He won't get away with this. We have rocks, a rope, two baseball bats, two torches, and an axe. That should be enough to stop him if he comes back.

But anything that can shred a tent like that must have really sharp teeth and claws. I suppose it could rip all four of us to shreds if it wanted to. Maybe we'll have to strike first.

"Where are those guys?" Stan asked.

"They've been gone for over half an hour."

"Maybe they decided to get more weapons," Jared said.

"They better not have wimped out," Stan said. "We need all the help we can get."

"They'll be back," Jared said. "Mitch wouldn't miss a challenge like this one."

In fact, Jared thought he could hear them now. There were footsteps coming up the path.

"Mitch?" Jared called.

There was no answer. But the steps were getting closer.

"Barry?" Stan called. "What's going on?"

The footsteps stopped. Someone was standing just beyond the light of the fire. Jared stood. He knew who it was.

"Nice night for a swim," he said sternly.

Rudy took a step closer. He was wearing the same clothes he'd had on at the pizza place. "Camping out again?" he said.

Jared reached down and grabbed a baseball bat for protection. "We would be," he said, "but it seems that something happened to our tent."

"Like what?" Rudy said.

"As if you don't know?" Jared said. "You ripped it up, didn't you?"

Rudy stepped back again. He looked at the baseball bat. Then he met Jared's eyes. "I didn't do anything to it."

"Sure, you didn't," Jared said.

"I didn't!" Rudy said loudly. "Why would I do something like that?"

"Because you're a werewolf."

Rudy laughed. "Where did you get a stupid idea like that?"

Jared gripped the bat tighter. "We saw you last night," he said. "Stalking through the woods. You dove into the pond as a wolf. Then you came up as you."

Rudy shook his head and frowned. "You guys are nuts," he said.

Stan was holding the axe. He jumped into the conversation. "You said you kill animals with your bare hands. You couldn't do that unless you were a werewolf. With sharp claws."

"Not true," Rudy said. "I'm a skilled hunter. But I'm not mean. I didn't touch your tent."

"Then who did?" Jared asked. "You say that you're such a great woodsman. You must have heard something."

"Sorry," Rudy said. "I didn't."

"You're a liar," Jared said. "And you owe me a hundred bucks for wrecking my tent."

Rudy shook his head. "I don't think so." He pointed to a torn pretzel bag on the ground. "You guys left food in the tent. Some animal smelled it and ripped through the tent to get it. A coyote would do that. Or a bear. Maybe even a raccoon."

Rudy turned and started to walk away.

"If you're such a great hunter, then why did you have to buy a meatball sandwich?" Stan called. "Couldn't kill enough rabbits?"

Rudy walked back toward the fire. "What are you talking about?" he said. "I didn't buy any sandwich."

"You know what he means," Jared said. "How can you deny that? We saw you at the Grotto this afternoon. We talked to you."

Rudy shook his head. "Not me. I never left the woods."

"Do you have a twin brother?" Stan asked.

"Nope."

"Then you're either crazy or you're lying," Jared said. "Either way, I don't trust anything you say. And I'm sure that you ruined my tent."

"I didn't," Rudy said calmly. "Believe what you want." Then he walked away.

"You'll pay for this!" Jared yelled. But

there was no response.

Jared stood and listened for several minutes. He felt sweat trickle down his forehead. He let out his breath. "What a jerk," he finally said.

The fire had started to die down. Jared threw on a few more pieces of wood.

"Do you think he really doesn't remember seeing us at the Grotto?" Stan asked.

"Who knows?" Jared replied. "Being a werewolf must affect your brain. So maybe he doesn't remember much."

"Maybe he doesn't remember wrecking the tent either," Stan said.

"Too bad," Jared said. "He did it. He owes me money."

"Good luck getting it," Stan said. "He won't be easy to track down."

Jared squatted and looked into the flames. "Where are Mitch and Barry?" he mumbled.

"Maybe the wolf got them," Stan said. He laughed. "Rudy the werewolf."

A long, loud howl came from the other side of the pond.

"There he is," Jared said. "The lying, tent-wrecking jerk."

Jared's Journal: Wednesday, August 4. 10:14 p.m.

So we sit here waiting. For what? For Mitch and Barry to return. For the full moon to rise. For more clues to what's going on. Is Rudy a total liar or is he losing his mind? Could he kill a rabbit? Could he kill us? Is he really a werewolf, or were our eyes playing tricks last night? We saw a big, ugly, four-legged creature. That I know is true. Was it a real wolf or a werewolf? Or was it something else?

Chapter 6:
Waiting

Mitch and Barry finally came back about a half hour later. They were laughing and making a lot of noise as they walked up the path.

"Quiet!" Jared said.

"What for?" Mitch said. "We're at least half a mile from anybody."

"What took you so long?" Jared asked. "Did you get more weapons?"

"Not exactly," Mitch said. He set a package on the ground. "We brought another tent." The orange tent was smaller than Jared's had been.

"That's tiny," Jared said.

"It's all we had in my garage," Mitch said. "It's my dad's. I didn't want to go into the house because my parents might have made me stay in. We can stash our stuff in it. We won't be sleeping anyway."

"We brought food, too," Barry said. He was carrying a bag filled with pretzels, potato chips, and popcorn.

Jared told them about the visit from Rudy. "He denied everything," Jared said. "He wouldn't even admit that he ate a meatball sandwich this afternoon."

"Yummy," said Barry. "Meatballs." He tore open the bag of potato chips. "Guess these will have to do."

"Were those in your garage too, Mitch?" Jared asked.

"Nah," Mitch said. "We stopped at a convenience store."

"You guys were gone for more than an hour," Jared said sharply. "We came face to face with the werewolf while you were shopping for potato chips!"

"The werewolf or the boy?" Barry asked. "Did he have sharp claws and a lot of hair?"

"Same guy," Jared said. "And no, he hadn't transformed yet. But wait until the moon comes up. I think we'll see a real werewolf then."

"Real werewolves don't eat at the Grotto," Barry said. "Or maybe they do. I guess a human could act normally during the day and turn into a werewolf at night."

"That's exactly what they do," Stan said.

Mitch started to spread out the tent. It was easy to assemble. He had it standing in a few minutes. Then he crawled in. "Wake me up when something happens!" he called.

"You can't sleep now," Jared said. "This is serious."

"I was just kidding," Mitch said. "Come

on in. There's room for everybody if we sit. We can tell horror stories."

"We're living a horror story," Jared said. "I'm staying out here to keep watch."

"Enjoy the mosquitoes," Mitch said.

Stan and Barry joined Mitch in the tent. They kept their flashlights on.

The fire was low again, but Jared let it be. It would burn for a long time yet. Jared liked it when it was mostly coals. It

gave just a little bit of heat and light. He sat close enough to avoid the bugs.

The trees in this area of the cemetery were mostly tall pines. Millions of insects were buzzing and chirping in the forest. Jared could hear a bullfrog croaking in the pond.

He stood and walked away from the tent so he could hear the sounds better. The sky was filled with stars.

This is what I love about the graveyard, Jared thought. *It's so peaceful out here at night. I don't want some killer werewolf spoiling all of this.*

He walked a few more steps. He couldn't see the pond down the hill. But he could smell it.

Jared yawned. He hadn't slept much last night. He didn't expect to sleep at all tonight.

We'll just wait until something happens, he told himself. *If Rudy is a werewolf, he'll definitely change when the moon comes up.*

Jared turned on his flashlight. He shined it toward the pond. The water looked very calm. He decided to take a closer look.

As he walked downhill to the pond, he could hear Mitch, Stan, and Barry laughing in the tent. He wished they'd be more serious about this. But he knew that he could count on them.

There might be some werewolf tracks in the mud, Jared thought. But the flashlight didn't show any. He could see sneaker prints. Probably his and Stan's.

Jared climbed onto a boulder and sat down. He turned off the light. *I thought I'd be more scared. This isn't so bad.*

A branch snapped in the woods. Jared looked around. All seemed calm.

Another snap. Jared squeezed the flashlight. But he didn't turn it on. Was something sneaking up on him?

Jared held his breath. He didn't blink.

He listened hard. All of those bugs were still buzzing.

Lots of things move in the forest, he thought. Most of them are harmless.

Jared breathed out. He looked around, but it was too dark. How could a person live out here all summer? Jared spent a lot of time in these woods. He hadn't seen another tent. He hadn't smelled a cooking fire. Rudy wasn't telling the truth.

But Rudy was out here tonight. And he'd been out here last night, too. So maybe that part of the story was true. But didn't Rudy have a family? Didn't someone wonder where he was? He was too young to be living on his own.

Jared looked up at the stars again. That made him feel calmer.

The other guys were about fifty yards away. Right up that hill. But maybe that was too far. Jared knew he'd better get back up there.

He stepped off the boulder and started up the hill.

And then he felt a hand take hold of his arm.

Chapter 7:
A Sharp Mind

"Hey!" Jared yelled. He shook his arm, but Rudy held tight.

"Shhh," said Rudy.

"Let go of my arm!"

Rudy let go. "I just wanted to talk to you," he said. "I need to talk to someone."

"About what?"

Rudy turned away. He seemed to be looking across the pond. There was a break in the trees there.

"Are you looking for the moon?" Jared asked.

Rudy nodded. He looked very sad.

"It won't be up for a while yet," Jared said.

"That's good," Rudy replied. "Strange things happen when the moon is up."

"To you?" Jared asked.

"To everything."

Jared folded his arms. He looked up the hill toward the tent. Should he yell for the others? Not yet.

"So what did you want to say?" Jared asked.

"I wanted to ask you something," Rudy said. "What did you guys mean about that meatball sandwich? You think you saw me downtown this afternoon?"

"You know that we saw you," Jared said. "How can you deny it?"

Rudy looked at the ground. Then he wiped his mouth with his hand. "I don't remember," he said. "I don't know what I did today."

Jared sneered. "You can't remember something that happened a few hours ago?"

Rudy shook his head. "It's been like that lately. At night, my thoughts are pretty clear. I feel alive. I can hunt down a rabbit and catch it with my bare hands. But during the day, it's like I'm sleepwalking."

"Every day?"

"For at least a week."

This guy is nuts, Jared thought. He started to walk. Rudy grabbed his arm again. Jared shook it off.

"What about before?" Jared asked. "Before the sleepwalking started. Did you live in the woods then?"

"I don't remember!" Rudy said. "I don't know where I lived or anything. I just found myself here in this graveyard about eight days ago. I don't remember anything before that."

"You don't remember if you have a family?"

Rudy was quiet for a moment. He seemed to be thinking hard. "I don't know," he said.

"You must have parents," Jared said. "How old are you?"

Rudy shrugged. "I'm not sure."

"How can you not know how old you are?"

Rudy looked confused. "I'm sure I used to know," he said. "Like I told you, parts of my mind are a blank."

"You said you're sharp at night."

"I am."

"Well, it's night now," Jared said. "You don't seem sharp at all."

Rudy looked toward the sky again. He blew out his breath.

"Are you a werewolf?" Jared asked.

"Me?"

"Yes, you," Jared said. "We heard a wolf last night. We saw it. And a few seconds later we heard it dive into the pond."

Rudy pointed toward the water. "That pond?"

"Of course, that pond."

"That's where I swim," Rudy said. "I mean, it's where I clean up."

"After you kill things?"

"Yes," Rudy said. "I have to eat, don't I?"

Jared nodded. "You didn't answer my question."

"Which one?"

"Are you a werewolf?"

Rudy shook his head. "I've been living like a wild animal," he said. "But if there's a werewolf out here, it isn't me."

"How can you be sure?" Jared asked. "You said you don't remember much. You can't even remember a meatball sandwich."

"That was during the day," Rudy said. "At night my mind is sharp. Most of the time, anyway. I think I'd know if I was a werewolf."

"Maybe not," Jared said. "If your body became a wolf, then your mind would, too."

"And I wouldn't remember?"

"Who knows?" Jared said. "I've never known a werewolf before. I don't know how they think. Maybe you got bit by one and don't remember."

Rudy looked at the break between the trees again. "What time is it?" he asked.

"Just after eleven."

"And what time will the moon be up?" Rudy asked.

"Around twelve o'clock, I think," Jared replied.

Rudy shook his head and folded his arms tight. "Maybe it will get cloudy."

"Not likely," Jared said. He pointed to the stars. There were very few clouds in the sky. "Did you think the clouds would block the moon?"

"I hoped so," Rudy said.

"What happens to you when the moon comes up?" Jared asked. He knew the answer. Rudy turned into a werewolf.

"I don't know," Rudy said.

"You said you remembered everything at night."

"Not everything," Rudy said. "When it's totally dark, I'm fine. But when the moon is up, things change."

"You are a werewolf," Jared said. He started walking faster up the path. Halfway up, he turned his flashlight beam back toward Rudy. But Rudy was gone.

Mitch, Stan, and Barry were still in the tent, talking softly. Jared put some more wood on the fire and sat next to it. The flames got bigger. Jared took out his notebook again.

Jared's Journal: Thursday, August 5.
12:04 a.m.
    A new day. A new night actually.

And the full moon is about to rise.

Rudy seems okay when he's human. He's scared and confused. But what happens next? How much danger are we in? And what will we do if he changes to a wolf and attacks? Does the water make a difference? Last night he dove in as a wolf and surfaced as Rudy. I've never heard that a werewolf can be changed back to a human by water. But who knows? There aren't any rules about these things.

I should have been afraid when I was talking to him. But I wasn't. He seemed harmless. But that might change in a little while. We need to prepare the torches, the bats, and the fire. I need to get those guys out of the tent soon to get ready.

We've got a battle on our hands.

Chapter 8:
RUN!

Jared sat by the fire for a while. Stan finally stuck his head out of the tent. "How's it going out here?" he asked.

"Okay," Jared said. "I had another talk with the werewolf."

Stan crawled out. He dropped a few sticks on the coals. A small flame shot up.

"What did he say?" Stan asked.

"Get Mitch and Barry," Jared said. "I'll fill you all in." But then he heard snoring from the tent.

"They fell asleep," Stan said. "I'll wake them."

"No, let them sleep," Jared said.

Jared and Stan decided to take a look around the area while Jared filled Stan in. They knew this spot well, but they might need to find some escape routes. That could be hard in the dark.

They brought the torches but didn't light them. Jared had matches in case they needed to use the torches to protect themselves.

They walked slowly through the forest. Jared told Stan about his latest talk with Rudy.

Soon they reached a ring of gravestones. The stones were small, only a foot or so tall. All of them were the same, and they circled a larger monument.

"This is the Civil War area," Jared said. "There isn't anyone buried here. These stones are in memory of men who never came back from the war."

He shined his flashlight on one of the stones. It said PVT. JAMES BALDWIN.

"Private?" Stan asked.

"Yeah."

Jared shut off his light. He'd heard some steady footsteps in the woods.

"Who's there?" he asked. "Rudy?"

Jared stepped closer to the large monument. He took the matches from his pocket, ready to light the torch.

"Let's walk," he said.

They went down the hill. Jared was aware of the footsteps again. Each time he stopped, the footsteps did too.

"We're being followed," Jared whispered.

"I know," Stan replied. "But we know who it is. Nobody else would be out here tonight except Rudy."

Then they heard a low growl.

Jared felt his stomach tighten. His skin

felt cold. "If that's Rudy, he's already changed into a wolf," he said. He looked at the sky. There was no sign of the moon yet.

Stan swept his flashlight beam into the woods. Whatever was following them was too far away to be seen.

"Why did we leave Mitch and Barry?" Jared said. "We'll need everybody if that wolf attacks."

"Let's work our way back," Stan said.

But the growl had come directly from the path that led to the tent. "We'll have to circle around," Jared said. He waved his hand toward a steeper section of woods. It was rocky and full of thorny bushes. "Through there."

"That will be dangerous in the dark," Stan said.

"More dangerous than a werewolf?" Jared said. "I don't think so."

They were only a few hundred yards

from the tent. But it took a long time to travel through the woods. They had their flashlights on, but they kept slipping. Jared bumped his knee on a rock. Both boys got cuts from the thorns.

And all the while, they could hear the wolf. It growled a few times. It stayed behind them, but it didn't get closer. They hadn't seen it yet. But they knew it was there.

Jared was sweating. He wasn't warm, but he was scared. "Should we light the torches?" he asked.

"I don't think so," Stan said. "Once they burn up, they're done. We might need them later."

"Let's rest," Jared said. He leaned against a tree. He couldn't hear the wolf any longer. Had it run off? Or was it sneaking closer?

"Rudy?" Jared said loudly. "If that's you, knock it off."

There was no reply.

Jared turned to Stan. "Should we wait here until the moon comes up?" he asked. "We'll see better."

"That's too long," Stan said. "But it looks like Rudy changes to a wolf at night whether the moon is out or not."

"It seems that way," Jared said. "But maybe the moon will have an effect, too. He might get meaner. He might attack."

"And we might get bitten," Stan said. "We'd better find our way back to the tent."

Jared let out his breath hard. "That tent won't protect us at all," he said. "Rudy will shred it like he did the other one."

"Right," Stan said. "But we have weapons there. And two more guys."

Another scream made them turn. This one sounded human.

"Help!" was the cry. "Help me!"

"That's Rudy!" Jared said.

"He turned back to a human?"

"He must have," Jared said. "But why's he screaming?"

"Hey, Rudy!" Stan yelled. "What's wrong?"

"The wolf's chasing me!" Rudy yelled.

They could hear hissing and growling. And they could hear loud, frantic footsteps.

"What do we do?" Jared asked.

"Head to the tent for help," Stan said. "We'll be safe while the wolf is chasing Rudy. Let's get Mitch and Barry. And the weapons."

They reached the tent as quickly as they could. Jared was bleeding from some new cuts on his arms.

Mitch and Barry were outside the tent, holding all of the weapons and the rope. They'd built the fire high.

"What's all the yelling?" Mitch asked.

"Rudy's in trouble," Jared said. "Let's go."

"Rudy the person or Rudy the wolf?"

Barry asked.

Stan shook his head. "It looks like Rudy isn't a werewolf after all. The wolf was chasing him. I hope we're not too late."

The shouting and growling had stopped. "I hope that wolf didn't catch Rudy for dinner," Barry said.

They hurried to the spot where they'd heard the shouting. Everything seemed quiet.

And then they heard Rudy's voice.

"Up here!" he said.

"Where?" Jared called. All four boys were searching with their flashlights.

"In the tree!" Rudy shouted.

Jared aimed his light halfway up a maple tree. Rudy was standing on a branch, hugging the trunk.

"It almost got me," Rudy said. "That wolf was five feet away when I reached this tree. If I hadn't grabbed a branch and pulled myself up, it would have bitten me."

"Where did it go?" Stan asked.

"It stayed below the tree for a few minutes," Rudy said. "Then it slinked off. But it probably didn't go far. Be careful."

Jared was holding a baseball bat. Mitch had the other one. Barry had the axe, and Stan had the rope and some rocks. Jared and Stan also had the unlit torches.

"We should make another fire right here," Mitch said. "That would keep the werewolf away while Rudy climbs down."

"No," Stan said. "One fire is enough. The woods are dry. We don't want to start a forest fire."

"There's no sign of the wolf anyway," Jared said. He shined his light on Rudy. "Or maybe there is."

Rudy climbed to a lower branch. Then he jumped to the ground. He was panting. "This close," he said, spreading his arms wide. "That's how close the wolf got to me. I could smell its breath. I'd be dead if

I'd been a second slower."

"You're safe now," Barry said.

"You think so?" Rudy asked with a sneer. "That wolf is around here somewhere. It's fast and fierce. And hungry. It could kill all five of us in a minute if it wanted to."

"What should we do?" Stan asked.

"We need to get somewhere safer," Rudy said. "I'm fast, like I told you. But that wolf would track you guys down without any problem. It would shred you like it did that tent."

Chapter 9:
Increased Danger

The four Zombie Hunters and Rudy walked quickly back toward the campsite. They kept their lights on, pointing them toward any sound. But there was no sign of the wolf.

"I guess we had you wrong," Stan said to Rudy. "We were sure you were a werewolf."

"I told you I wasn't," Rudy said.

Jared tapped Mitch on the shoulder. He motioned for him to stay back. Mitch would understand what Jared had to say.

When the others were twenty yards ahead, Jared spoke softly. "We still haven't seen Rudy and the wolf at the same time," he said.

"We haven't?"

"No," Jared said. "We heard Rudy yelling. We heard an animal growling. But we don't have any real proof that Rudy isn't a werewolf. He could have made both sounds."

Mitch sighed. "I guess that's true."

Jared pointed to the break in the hills where the moon was rising. "Maybe we'll know soon," he said. "The moon will be up before long."

"What do you think will happen?" Mitch asked.

"I have no idea," Jared said. "We'll keep an eye on him. Watch to see if he changes. And keep the weapons close."

Rudy said he was hungry. He sat on the ground next to the fire and ate handfuls of pretzels and popcorn.

"No rabbits tonight?" Stan asked.

"Didn't have time," Rudy said. "I was starting to hunt when the wolf arrived."

"Are you sure there was a wolf?" Jared asked. "Not everything you say makes sense."

"It was chasing me!" Rudy exclaimed. "Didn't you hear it?"

"We heard a lot of hissing and growling," Jared said. "And we heard you yelling."

"It almost caught me," Rudy said.

Jared didn't know what to believe. He squeezed the baseball bat. He set it by his feet and took out his notebook.

Jared's Journal: Thursday, August 5. 12:53 a.m.

The sky is growing brighter. We'll have moonlight soon. Is Rudy a werewolf? Or is he just some crazy guy with no memory? Is there a real wolf running loose in this cemetery? Or another werewolf? What was *chasing Rudy? Or was NOTHING chasing Rudy? This is all very strange. I'm starting to think that maybe*

"He's gone!" Stan yelled.

Jared dropped his pen. "Who's gone?" he said.

"Rudy! He was here ten seconds ago."

All of the flashlights went on. Rudy was not in sight.

"Everybody hold still," Jared said. But they couldn't hear anything.

"Where did he go?" Mitch said. "Rudy!"

"Did he take anything?" Jared said. "Do we have all the weapons?"

"The rope is gone," Stan said. "Nothing else."

Jared had figured that they'd be safe if they kept Rudy close by. If he started to change into a wolf, they would tie him up until he changed back. It was for his own good. And also for their safety.

Now Rudy had fled. The danger had increased.

"How did you let him get away?" Jared said. "That was really stupid."

"Don't blame us," Barry said. "You didn't stop him either."

"I was busy," Jared said. "I was working out a plan." He bent down and picked up his pen. "This is crazy."

"I'll tell you what else is crazy," Mitch said. "Look!" He pointed to the break between the hills. The full moon was coming up. But it was orange.

"There must be some smog," Jared said. "The moon often looks orange when it's low in the sky. It's from the light hitting clouds or pollution."

"Does an orange moon have the same effect on a werewolf?" Mitch asked.

"We'll find out," Jared said. "But I'm sure it does."

"This is not good," Stan said. "We're in

danger of attack from two creatures now. A real wolf and a werewolf."

"Or maybe not," Jared said. "I have an idea about all this. But we need to be alert. Keep your weapons handy. Build up that fire again. And don't wander off, no matter what. We need all four of us at our best. Fighting off a man is one thing. Dealing with a crazed animal is something else."

Chapter 10:
The Wolf Knows

Jared wiped some blood from his arm. He was still bleeding from the thorns.

"That blood might attract the wolf," Stan said. "You should clean it off."

Jared shrugged. "The wolf knows where we are," he said. "A little bit of blood won't matter."

The four boys were standing close together. Their backs were toward the fire. Every sound from the forest seemed louder now. Every movement sounded like danger.

"What do you think Rudy is doing with our rope?" Mitch asked.

"I have no idea," Jared said.

"Maybe he'll hang it from a tree so he can climb faster," Stan said. "In case that wolf chases him again."

Jared looked up at the treetops. "Maybe we'd be safer in a tree, too," he said.

"I'd rather stay down here with our weapons," Stan said.

"And the fire," Mitch added.

Jared was still trying to figure out what was going on. Had Rudy made all that noise by himself? The yelling and the growling? Had he climbed the tree so the boys would think he'd been chased?

Or was there really a wolf out there in the dark? Or some other creature that was even more deadly?

They were all quiet for a few minutes. Jared thought he heard a growl. He thought he heard footsteps. But he wasn't sure of anything.

"I just remembered something," Mitch said. "A few years ago in Maine, a strange animal got killed by a car. It looked something like the wolf you described last night."

"What was it?" Jared asked.

"It turned out to be a very big, wild dog," Mitch said. "But people had been seeing it for years. It had killed sheep and pets. They said it was dark gray, with big fangs and evil eyes."

"I read about that," Barry said. "It had a chilling howl. They thought it was a mix of a dog and a wolf, or maybe a coyote. It seemed to be some kind of mutant. It was insane and would kill anything."

"That could be what we're dealing with," Jared said. "Wolves are very rare here. But dogs and coyotes aren't. Sometimes they breed."

"They said it had a cry that would send

chills up your spine," Mitch said.

"We heard a howl like that last night," Stan said. "From over near the pond."

"Let's just listen," Jared said.

The only nearby sounds were the crackling of the fire and the buzzing of the insects. But then they did hear a howl. It sounded far away.

"Do you think that's Rudy?" Stan asked.

Jared didn't answer. He could hear another sound. Something was moving very slowly in the forest just a few yards away.

"Get ready," Jared said. "It's coming."

"What is?" Mitch whispered.

"Just listen."

There were big gaps between the sounds. But everyone heard them. Something was taking careful steps. Trying not to be heard. Getting closer.

"Let's light the torches," Jared said. He and Stan dipped the ends of their torches into the fire. They began to burn.

The torches made a lot of light. With Mitch and Barry holding flashlights, the boys could see into the woods. But they didn't see whatever was coming. And they heard no more footsteps.

"It's the werewolf," Barry said. "I know it."

Jared didn't dare blink. He scanned the forest. His lips felt dry and his heart was racing. He knew that the creature must be staring right at him. But Jared didn't know where it was.

They heard a snort. Then a low growl. It came from the edge of the woods, perhaps forty feet away.

"The moon's way up now," Mitch said. "I think it's Rudy. He's changed into a wolf."

Jared swallowed hard. He tried to work up some spit, but his mouth was too dry. He gripped his torch tighter.

"I think we should get out of here," Barry said. "Get to safety."

"I don't think we can," Jared said. "Whatever is out there is waiting to pounce. At least if we stay here we'll see it coming. We can fight it off."

Barry pointed to Jared's torch. "That won't burn much longer," he said. "Then what will we do?"

Jared thought for a moment. There hadn't been any new footsteps. The creature must be close enough to attack. He lowered his torch and moved it in a circle, trying to shine more light into the woods.

And then he saw the eyes. They were glowing yellow. The creature was about twenty feet away.

"Get your weapons!" Jared yelled.

The creature stared right back at Jared. But Jared could only see the eyes. They were about two feet above the ground. It was a four-footed animal. Probably the same one they'd seen the night before.

The creature hissed.

Stan spoke up. "Listen, Rudy," he said loudly, "if you can control this, then turn back to a human. Do it now!"

The torches were growing dim. Mitch and Barry kept their flashlight beams on the yellow eyes. The creature started to back up.

And then it charged the boys!

Jared dove to the side as the creature lunged past him. It leaped over the campfire. Its tail dragged in the coals. Sparks shot up.

Stan swung his torch at the animal, but didn't hit it. Mitch and Barry rolled on the ground. The animal roared and ran into the woods.

Jared could hear it crashing through the forest. It whined and howled. It was running fast, away from the boys.

"Why did it do that?" Stan asked. "Was it just trying to scare us?"

"If it was trying to scare us, it worked," Jared said. His hands were shaking.

"Did you see how big its mouth was?" Mitch asked. "It would bite your arm off in one shot."

"Big, sharp fangs," Barry said. "And huge paws. I didn't see its claws, but I'll bet they were sharp as knives."

The animal was bigger than Jared thought it would be. It was nearly all black. Its eyes were shiny.

Jared felt numb. "That thing could have killed us if it wanted to," he said.

"It doesn't have to kill us," Stan said. "One bite is all it takes. Then we'd be werewolves, too."

"Was that the same creature you saw last night?" Mitch asked.

"It looked bigger tonight," Jared said. "But that's probably because it was so close."

"Do you think it was a wolf?" Barry asked. "I've never seen one up close. But that looked like some kind of mutant."

Stan picked up a stick and poked at the fire. The animal's tail had spread the coals. Stan pushed them back together. He added more wood. Soon the flames were back.

Jared stepped closer to the fire. The creature howled, but it sounded far away.

"It sounds like a wolf," Jared said. "But I agree. It didn't look like a normal animal at all."

And then they heard Rudy yell. It was a loud "Ahhh!" He didn't sound scared. Just loud.

"What's that all about?" Mitch asked.

"Rudy's crazy," Jared said. "And he knows he can scare us. Let's not let him."

"Too late," Stan said. "I'm already scared. We all are. This is a dangerous situation. We've got an unknown creature that could kill us in a second. And a crazy guy who might be a werewolf. That's a bad combination. We need to get out of here."

"I agree," Barry said. "We can't handle this."

"Yes, we can," Mitch said. "We're the Zombie Hunters. We've faced all kinds of nasty ghouls before. We can deal with these, too."

"How?" Stan asked. "We're not safe here. Especially in the dark. Rudy and that creature keep sneaking up on us. The only thing keeping us safe is the fire."

"Then we should stay by it," Jared said. "Trying to leave the cemetery now would expose us even more."

"Let's think this through," Mitch said. "We can stay here all night and hope for the best. Or we can try to escape. Or we can go after those two creatures and finish them off. Whatever we do, we're in danger."

"Big danger," said Barry. "The biggest we've ever faced."

Chapter 11:
Ow-oooooh

Jared's Journal: Thursday, August 5. 3:46 a.m.

It's been quiet for more than an hour now. Too quiet. When the insects stop buzzing and the small animals stop moving, you know that there's something wrong. It's because there's a monster out there. Lurking. And maybe a werewolf, too.

Barry and Stan couldn't take it. They left a half hour ago. They were certain that there were two dangers: Rudy and a wolf. I still think that's one danger. Rudy and the wolf are the same thing. That's dangerous enough for me.

I assume Barry and Stan made it out of the graveyard safely. We didn't hear an attack. We didn't hear them scream.

Now it's just Mitch and me.

Why did we stay? To protect this space. To try to get rid of the evil creatures. And because it's exciting. I have to admit that. As scary as this is, it gives me a thrill. What could be more interesting than testing your wits against the supernatural?

We've kept the fire roaring since Barry and Stan left. I keep yawning. Haven't really slept for two nights now.

"This is driving me crazy," Mitch said. "Just waiting. I'm too scared to sit down."

Jared put his notebook in his pocket. He

scratched at a bite on his arm. If he'd had to choose one person to stay with him, it would be Mitch. Mitch was tough and he was smart. And it took a lot to scare him.

The fire made strange shadows on the ground. Jared would usually feel very calm on a night like this. The moon was out and the air was still. But now he just wanted the night to end.

"This hasn't been a usual Zombie Hunters' mission," Mitch said. "We haven't had any success at all."

Jared sighed. "I don't even know what success would mean."

The Zombie Hunters had dealt with ghosts and other spirits many times in the past. But those things were already dead. When the boys drove them back to their graves, they were putting them back to rest. They weren't killing them.

But Rudy and the wolf were alive. Finishing them off didn't seem right at all.

"We can't kill them," Jared said. "Unless our lives are in danger."

"You're right," Mitch said. "We've figured out that Rudy is nuts. But he hasn't done anything to hurt us. So we can't hurt him. And we don't know much about that wolf."

"Or whatever it is," Jared said. He thought it might be a mix of some kind. Part wolf, part coyote? Part panther? Or was there a much bigger story than that? "Maybe it's some kind of zombie animal."

"I think it's a wolf," Mitch said. "It's not a normal wolf though. I feel sorry for it."

"Do you still think Rudy and the wolf are two different beings?" Jared asked.

"It seems that way," Mitch said. "Don't you think so?"

"We still haven't seen them at the same time," Jared replied. "I think Rudy is the werewolf. We're dealing with just one being. A very messed-up creature who takes on two different forms. Human and animal."

"But we've heard them at the same time."

"Maybe not," Jared said. He stared at the flames for a long while. "Rudy's not all there, you know what I mean? He has gaps in his memory. But he might be a very clever werewolf. The wolf side of him might be capable of switching from wolf to human whenever he wants to. And making sounds like both."

"But didn't the wolf chase Rudy up a tree?" Mitch asked. "Do you think that was all a trick?"

"It might have been," Jared said. "We didn't see it happen. We didn't see the wolf then. We just saw Rudy in the tree."

"It doesn't make sense."

"None of this does," Jared said. "Rudy is insane. I think some part of him wants to kill us. Or at least infect us. When he's in werewolf form, he can allow himself to try. But when he's a human, he won't allow himself do it. So he goes back and forth. And then he chickens out."

"So even when he's a wolf, he's thinking like a human?"

"Partly," Jared said. "And when he's a human, he's thinking like a wolf. But he doesn't remember everything he does."

"So how do we put an end to that?" Mitch asked.

"I don't know," Jared replied.

A few minutes later, Jared heard a sound that made him feel a little better. "Listen," he said. Birds were beginning to chirp. Just a few.

"They start at the first hint of dawn," Jared said. "We can't even detect the light yet. But they can."

"So the sun will be up soon?" Mitch asked.

"No. Not for an hour. But the birds know it's coming."

"It can't happen soon enough for me," Mitch said. "Stan and Barry were smart to leave when they did. Let's just survive this night and get out of here."

"That won't solve anything," Jared said.

"No," Mitch said. "But maybe this one is too much for us to solve. Maybe the Zombie Hunters are failing this time. That's better than being dead."

Jared looked around. He didn't want to give up this spot. He'd spent so many hours of his life in this cemetery. Riding his bike here. Climbing trees. Sledding down the hills in the winter. Camping out. This was like his second home.

How could he let the fear of a werewolf put this graveyard off-limits?

"We'll never be able to camp here again if we don't do something," Jared said.

Mitch rubbed his hands over the fire.

"It's always coldest before dawn," he said. Then he laughed. "Maybe Rudy turns into a wolf just to stay warm at night. All that hair."

Jared laughed, too. "And maybe it protects him from the mosquitoes."

"He's one crazy guy," Mitch said. Then he let a long, loud howl. "Ow-oooooh!"

Jared cracked up. And he howled, too.

And then there was a much louder howl. A real one.

Jared felt a chill. His hands grew damp.

"It's coming back," Mitch said.

"Grab the weapons," Jared said. "This is it!"

"Are we attacking?" Mitch asked.

"No," Jared said. "We're getting ready to defend ourselves again!"

Chapter 12:
Get Up the Tree

They could hear the creature running through the woods. It circled around them, then ran down the hill behind them. It was snorting and hissing.

"It's getting ready to charge," Jared said. He and Mitch were both holding baseball bats. They'd built the fire high. And they were shining their flashlights toward the sound.

"We need to get up a tree," Mitch said.

But the creature was very close again. It kept moving in a tighter circle. The boys could see it some of the time, but it stayed mostly in the dark.

They didn't dare leave the fire. Jared moved his light along the line of trees. None of them looked easy to climb. The closest trees were tall pines, and the branches were too high to reach.

"We really should have gone home when we had the chance," Mitch said.

"Too late now," Jared said.

The creature growled.

Jared set his flashlight at his feet. He picked up a rock. He couldn't see the creature, but he could hear its loud breathing.

Jared threw the rock with all his might. He heard it hit a tree and bounce away. But he also heard the creature take a few quick steps back.

"You scared it," Mitch said. He picked up a rock and threw it, too. After several more throws, they heard the creature bound away.

"We scared it off," Mitch said.

"Not for long. It will be back for sure."

"I'm not waiting any longer," Mitch said. "Head toward the pond. We'll climb the first easy tree we find. Then we'll wait up there until daylight."

They rushed down the path.

A voice cried, "Better hurry!" It was Rudy.

"Where are you?" Jared called.

But Rudy didn't answer.

"You'd better find a safe place!" Mitch called. "That creature just ran past us."

Jared and Mitch kept running.

And then the wolf charged down the hill.

Jared ran right. Mitch ran left.

Jared leaped for a tree branch. He gripped it with both hands and swung his legs up. Then he climbed to the next branch. And the next. Soon he was high above the pond. He yelled for Mitch.

"Are you okay?"

"Not quite," Mitch said. "I smashed my arm against a tree. I hurt my leg, too."

Jared could tell that Mitch wasn't far away. "Where's the wolf?" he asked.

"I don't know," Mitch said. "I don't hear it."

"You'd better climb," Jared said. "Can you?"

"I think so," Mitch said.

"That wolf must be close by," Jared said. "Get up in a tree."

Jared could hear Mitch struggling to climb. "Easy does it," Jared called. "Did you lose your light?"

"Yeah," Mitch said. "I dropped it when the wolf charged."

"Me, too. I threw it. I don't think it hit the wolf though." Jared clung to the tree trunk. The moon gave a bit of light, but it was hard to see much.

Jared's hands were bleeding from

scrambling up the tree. And he was breathing hard.

Settle down, he told himself. *Just a little while longer until daylight.*

He heard movement in the water and looked down. Something big was swimming. "Can you see that, Mitch?"

"No."

"Are you in a tree?" Jared asked.

"Partway up."

"How's your arm?"

"It's okay," Mitch said.

Jared watched the water. He was sure he'd heard something. But the water seemed still.

Then something broke the surface in the center of the pond. Was it the wolf?

No, it was Rudy. And he started singing again.

"Are you crazy?" Mitch called. "The wolf's down there. Get out of the water."

"What wolf?"

"What do you mean, 'what wolf?'" Mitch said. "The wolf that's been chasing us all night."

"There's a wolf chasing us?"

Jared couldn't believe what he was hearing. Rudy was definitely insane. He couldn't even remember things that had happened a half hour before.

Now Jared was certain that Rudy was the wolf. The wolf had chased him and Mitch. It had been right here. Now the wolf was gone and Rudy was in the pond. He had changed back to a human.

And he would probably change back to a wolf very soon.

I'm staying in this tree, Jared thought. *It's the only safe place in the cemetery.*

Rudy swam beneath the surface of the water. This time, Jared didn't see him come up.

Chapter 13:
Crash!

"Mitch?" Jared called after a few minutes.

"Yeah?" It sounded as if Mitch was about thirty yards away.

"Do you see anything?"

"Not much."

"Me either," Jared said. "I don't hear the wolf. Or Rudy."

"Are you still convinced that they're the same being?"

"Yes," Jared said. "If not, I think the wolf would have got him this time. It chased us. And then it was gone. And now here's Rudy in the pond. He's swimming like there's no danger at all."

"He's gone now."

Jared shifted a bit. He was sitting on a thick branch. He had his arms wrapped around the tree trunk. Bugs were biting his arms, legs, and neck. But he didn't dare slap at them. He held tight so he wouldn't fall.

It was a long way down.

"Rudy!" Mitch yelled.

There was no reply.

"He was swimming," Jared said. "Did you see him leave the water?"

"No," Mitch said. "But he's a good swimmer."

"He's also losing his mind," Jared said.

Jared stared at the moon's reflection on the pond. Suddenly it grew darker. He looked up at a thick cloud. It was blocking the moon.

"Are you bleeding?" Jared called.

"A little," Mitch said. "Not much. You?"

"No more than before," Jared said.

He sat quietly for several minutes. His notebook was on the ground somewhere back at the campsite. He imagined what he would write in it if he could.

Jared's Journal: Thursday, August 5. Just before dawn.

This is the calmest time of the night. Or is it the creepiest? I don't know how to get out of this one. I could climb down the tree and just walk away. Maybe a crazed wolf would kill me. Or maybe there's no such thing right now. Just a weird guy named Rudy. Maybe he drowned. Maybe he turned back into a wolf.

Maybe I'm the one who's crazy. After all, I'm clinging to a tree trunk at 4:30 in the morning. I'm bleeding and starving and I haven't slept for two nights. And I'm risking my life up here. For what?

Jared heard something moving near the base of the tree. It was too dark to see what was there.

"Rudy?" Jared said.

All was quiet again. Jared thought he could hear something breathing. Then he heard it rubbing against the tree trunk.

"Mitch?" Jared called.

"What?"

"Are you still in that tree?"

"Of course."

"Rudy?" Jared said again.

It had to be Rudy. But was it Rudy the human or Rudy the wolf? Maybe it didn't matter. The wolf was a bigger danger, but Jared didn't trust the human either. The human was sick. Rudy didn't even know who he was anymore.

There was more rubbing. Then a shifting sound, like something starting to climb the tree. Jared could hear claws trying to grip the bark.

"Mitch?" Jared called.

"Yeah?"

"Wolves can't climb trees, right?"

"I don't think so," Mitch said.

But something was climbing the tree. It was moving very slowly. Jared couldn't see it. But he heard it.

"Maybe a werewolf can climb," Mitch said.

Jared reached up. The next branch was pretty high. But he needed to get there. Whatever was climbing the tree was getting closer.

I can't believe this, Jared thought. *This seemed like the safest spot in the cemetery.*

Jared pulled some sticks and leaves from the branch and tossed them down. He heard them hit the ground. So he did it again. This time he hit something. It was alive. It snarled.

"Something's climbing my tree!" Jared

called. "Can you see what it is?"

"It's too dark," Mitch yelled back. "Rudy! Is that you?"

"Get lost, Rudy!" Jared shouted. "Leave us alone."

But Jared could hear the animal creeping closer. He reached for the higher branch and pulled himself up. The leaves were thicker here. The branch was thinner. He was nearly to the top of the tree. He couldn't go any higher.

The edge of the pond was about forty feet below him. Way too far to jump. He knew that the water was fairly deep in the middle of the pond. But he would drop straight down into shallow water. From this height it would be very dangerous. He would hit bottom. He might break a leg. Or worse.

There was more clawing at the trunk. He could see a dark shape nearing the branch he'd just left behind. It didn't look like a human. It looked like the wolf!

Jared reached for more leaves to throw. His hand gripped something tough. It was the rope! The end was knotted and wrapped around the branch. The rest of the rope hung down toward the pond. Rudy must have climbed up here with it. He'd set it up as an escape route.

It might be Jared's only way out.

"Mitch!" Jared yelled. "That thing is right below me! Can you see it yet?"

"No," Mitch said. "But I'm climbing down. I'll throw rocks at it."

"Stay there!" Jared said. "You'd be a sitting duck on the ground. It didn't climb up very quickly, but I'd bet it could get down fast. You'd never escape."

Jared could hear it growling now. He could see its evil, yellow eyes. He slid a bit farther out on the branch. But the wolf would be upon him in seconds.

The branch cracked. It didn't break, but

Jared knew that it wouldn't hold his weight much longer. If the wolf came out here, it would break for sure.

Jared looked up. The top branches were much too thin to hold his weight. He had nowhere else to go. He took hold of the rope with one hand and held the branch with the other.

The wolf roared. It swiped a paw toward Jared. The branch cracked louder. Jared gripped the rope with both hands. He swung out over the pond as far as he could.

He fell through the air for what seemed like forever. The tension of the rope finally held. Jared dangled about ten feet above the pond. Then, he heard a snap and the branch let loose. Jared hit the water with a splash.

He began kicking his legs and thrashing his arms. The water closed over his head. It smelled like fish and dead plants. The water was cold. He plunged down deep but didn't hit bottom. Then he burst to the surface.

"Whoa!" he yelled, gasping for air. He looked around quickly. Was the wolf in the pond with him? Was it still in the tree?

"Are you all right?" Mitch shouted.

"Yeah! Where's the wolf?"

"It crashed," Mitch yelled. "I'm on my way down."

Jared began to swim. After a few quick strokes, he reached shallow water. He waded the rest of the way out.

A light went on. "I found my flashlight," Mitch said. "It never went out. Are you sure you're okay?"

"Yes." Jared felt his arms and legs. Nothing hurt except his hands, which had been burned by the rope. "You said it crashed?"

"Didn't you hear it?"

"I was underwater," Jared said.

Mitch had his light aimed at a boulder

below the tree. The creature was lying there. It was motionless.

"It made a racket when it was falling," Mitch said. "Howling and roaring. But it stopped cold when it hit that rock. It made a huge thud. I heard bones breaking, too."

"One of us was going to die," Jared said. "It was it or me. That thing was inches away from me. And it wanted blood."

Chapter 14:
Gruesome Discovery

Jared felt sick. The creature was lying lifeless on the boulder. Its skull was broken. Blood was seeping from its ears and its mouth.

They stepped closer. The animal's coat was thick and black. It had solid leg muscles and sharp claws. It seemed to be in good health. But its head was very small for the size of its body. Its yellow eyes were set back too far. Its mouth was wider than it should have been.

"The whole head is deformed," Mitch

said. "Even before it got smashed against the rock, I mean. This is not a normal animal. No wonder it was insane. Its brain must have been pinched inside that little head."

"I know," Jared said. "But I hate to see anything die like that. What a brutal fall."

And then Jared had another thought. This wasn't just a deformed animal. It might be Rudy. If Rudy really was a dead werewolf, then his human form was dead, too.

"We need to report this," Jared said. "We should go to the police station."

Mitch nodded. "Okay," he said. "But let's wait a few minutes. I need to calm down. I'm shaking."

They sat on another boulder and stared at the creature. "Maybe a scientist can figure out what kind of creature that was," Jared said. "It's not anything I've ever seen."

"Not many people get a chance to see a

werewolf," Mitch said.

Jared took off his shirt and wrung it out. He was cold, but his heart was pumping so hard that he barely noticed the chill.

They walked slowly into town. Mitch was limping. Jared's hands stung.

When they reached Main Street, a poster caught Jared's eye.

"Look at this," Jared said. The small yellow poster was taped to the front window of the bagel shop. It said MISSING TEEN. And it had a photograph of Rudy!

MISSING TEEN
Rudy Welker, Age 15
5-foot-7, 135 pounds
Last seen at home in Waterboro on July 26.

Rudy is harmless, but he has an illness and needs daily medication. If you know his location, please call the Waterboro police.

Jared swallowed hard. He felt awful for Rudy. He wasn't just missing. He was dead.

"Waterboro is about twenty miles from here," Jared said.

"At least we know who to contact," Mitch said. "But it'll be sad news. Let's tell the Marshfield cops. They can pick up Rudy's body and let the Waterboro police know."

Jared grabbed Mitch's arm. "Wait a minute," he said. "The body is a wolf. No one will believe that it's Rudy."

"You're right," Mitch said. "Maybe we'd better go back. He probably stashed his clothes and things somewhere near the pond. If we can find those, it would help identify Rudy."

"Want to grab a bagel first?" Jared said.

"The shop won't be open for another half hour," Mitch said.

"Should we wait? I'm starving. That

body won't be going anywhere."

But then Jared saw his reflection in the window of the bagel shop. His face was streaked with dirt. There was a long scratch on his forehead, and some drops of dried blood. His eyes were bloodshot from lack of sleep.

"I look like a monster," he whispered.

"I don't look much better," Mitch replied.

"I just remembered something else," Jared said. "We never put out the campfire."

"I'm sure it burned out by now," Mitch said.

"Probably. But I don't like leaving hot coals. That can be dangerous."

They hurried back to the graveyard. Jared wondered if a dead werewolf would turn back into a human when the sun came up. A live human, he hoped.

"What do you think?" Jared asked. "Do you think its human form survived?"

Mitch shut his eyes quickly and shook his head. "We'll soon find out," he said. "But I doubt it."

Jared's heart sank as they reached the top of the hill above the pond. He could see the boulder. The dead creature was still there.

Flies were buzzing around the creature's face, feeding on the blood. It made Jared very sad. Rudy was finished.

Mitch rubbed his chin. "I still say it's a werewolf."

"Maybe," Jared said. "Just in case, we'd better find the werewolf's clothes."

They searched the area near the pond. But they didn't find any of Rudy's things.

"Poor guy," Jared said. "Maybe the medicine kept him normal. But then he wandered away and got confused. Without the medicine, he barely knew who he was anymore."

"Let's get my tent," Mitch said. "Then

we'll alert the police."

"Let's just wait a minute," Jared said. He stared at the creature on the rock. It didn't look so dangerous now. He knew it had tried to kill him. But that had been the werewolf form. Not the human one.

Jared looked up at the pond. Stan's rope was floating in the middle. It had saved Jared's life. He wished that it somehow could have saved Rudy, too.

"Come on," Mitch said. "Let's kick some dirt over those hot coals."

As they headed up the hill, Jared could smell smoke. He heard a fire crackling.

"We might be too late," Jared said. He ran the rest of the way.

But the fire wasn't out of control. It was contained in the ring of stones. Someone had fed it with wood.

"Who's here?" Mitch asked.

There was snoring from the tent. Jared pulled back the flap.

Rudy was inside sleeping.

"He's alive!" Jared said. He shook Rudy's shoulder. He didn't wake up.

Mitch whistled. "So he wasn't a werewolf after all."

"I guess not," Jared said. He put his hand on Rudy's chest. His heart was beating. "The wolf is dead. Rudy is not."

"He must need his medicine badly," Mitch said. "Sounds like he hasn't had it this week."

"Rudy!" Jared said. He shook him again.

Rudy opened his eyes, but he didn't move.

"Rudy, you need help," Jared said. "Can you get up and walk?"

Rudy shook his head. He shut his eyes and went right back to sleep.

"He needs an ambulance," Jared said. He pointed toward his house. "You stay with him, Mitch. I'll go call. If he wakes up, just make sure he doesn't run off."

"I don't think he'll be going anywhere," Mitch said. "He's zonked out."

Jared ran as fast as he could. He had a lot of explaining to do. And he hoped someone could explain to him what that dead creature on the rock really was.

All of that could wait. For now he had to hurry. Rudy's life was at stake.

But he was glad to know that Rudy could still be saved.

Tracking a Werewolf
Tips from Jared Jensen

Step 1: Go to the woods to search for the werewolf. Keep your eyes peeled for big sets of paw prints.

Step 2: Once paw prints are found, scan the woods for evil, yellow eyes in the bushes.

Step 3: Listen for growling, howling, and hissing. These are all sounds made by a werewolf.

Step 4: Beware of bushes shaking and branches breaking, the werewolf could be tracking you.

Step 5: If stampeding sounds are coming your way, RUN!

Step 6: Climbing a tree can slow the attack, but werewolves can climb. They are slow, and it will give you a chance to get away.

Step 7: Get to safety.

Werewolf Facts
from Jared Jensen

#1: Werewolves don't sleep.

#2: Werewolves eat raw animals that they kill.

#3: Some werewolves can turn from human to wolf whenever they want.

#4: Some werewolves don't want to become wolves. It just happens. Like when the full moon comes up.

#5: Werewolves have a huge thirst for blood.

#6: Their sense of smell is strong. It is a hundred times better than a human's sense of smell.

#7: It's rumored werewolves can't climb trees. (But we learned differently!)

#8: Werewolves are dangerous because they move quickly and have great strength. Always be careful when exploring wooded areas.

ABOUT THE ...

Author

Baron Specter is the pen name
of Rich Wallace, who has
written many novels for kids and
teenagers. His latest books include
the Kickers soccer series and the
novel *Sports Camp*.

Illustrator

Setch Kneupper has years of
experience thinking he saw a ghost,
although Graveyard Diaries is the
first series of books he's illustrated
about the ordeal.